For Jasmine

First published 1993 by
Walker Books Ltd, 87 Vauxhall Walk
London SE11 5HJ

Text © 1993 Vivian French
Illustrations © 1993 John Prater

Printed and bound in Hong Kong by
South China Printing Co. (1988) Ltd

Brititsh Library Cataloguing in Publication Data
A catalogue record for this book
is available from the British Library.
ISBN 0-7445-2252-8

C70617919q

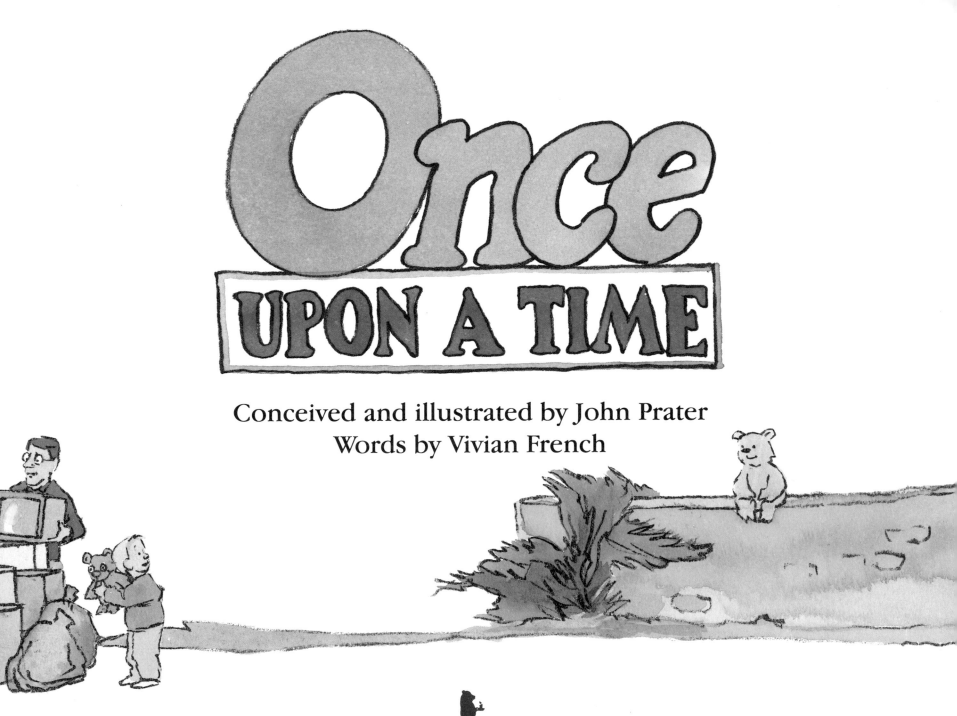

Once
UPON A TIME

Conceived and illustrated by John Prater
Words by Vivian French

WALKER BOOKS
LONDON

Early in the morning
Cat and me.
Not much to do.
Not much to see.

Dad's off to work now
Mum's up too.
Not much to see.
Not much to do.

Day's getting older
Sun's up high.
Wave to a little girl
Hurrying by.

Mum's cleaning windows.
Here's a bear
Making a fuss
About a chair.

Ride my tricycle
For a while.
There's an egg
With a happy smile.

Mum's in the garden.
Washing's dry.
Why do babies
Always cry?

We've got sandwiches –
Cheese today.
Why's that wolf saying
"Come this way"?

I like jumping
To and fro.
That wolf's howling
He's hurt his toe.

Mum's drinking coffee.
We can chat.
I tell her my jump
Is as big as THAT!

Here's Dad home again!
Time for tea.
I wave to him
And he waves to me.

Dad's washing dishes.
I look out.
Did I hear someone
Walking about?

Time for my story.
I yawn and say,
"Nothing much happened
Round here today."